I dedicate this book to my Dad for inspiring and encouraging me to share this story I wrote when I was a 14-year-old kid by convincing me to turn it into an illustrated book!

- Rea M. C. M.

Here comes a story about a time where
it was impossible for humans to walk.
As impossible as fish swimming.

Well, it's probably worth mentioning that
at this time, only the privileged birds swam.

The fish, they walked.

... and the humans?
The humans flew sky-high.

Humans tend to want what they can't have, so it would be safe to say that each living person, at some point in their life, wished they were able to walk.

However, no one could, and most would never dare to try.

That is until, one summer day, a naughty boy named Nathan flew out of his house only for an even naughtier idea to fly into his mind.

You see, Nathan was a super clever genius of a kid that devoted all his intelligence to annoying people as best he could.

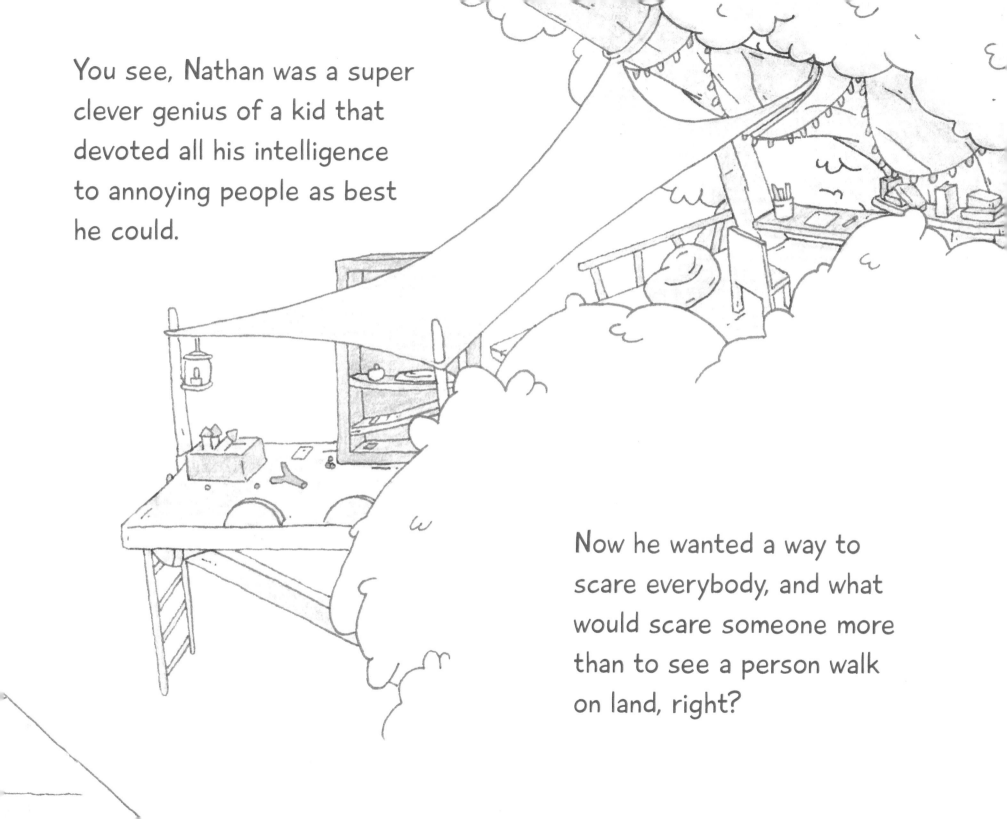

Now he wanted a way to scare everybody, and what would scare someone more than to see a person walk on land, right?

He gave it some thought, and when his plan was final, he was to narrate it to a fish, for he needed the help of a fish to carry out his seemingly brilliant plan.

He hovered down, as near land as he could, spotted a friendly-looking fish, and began explaining his plan.

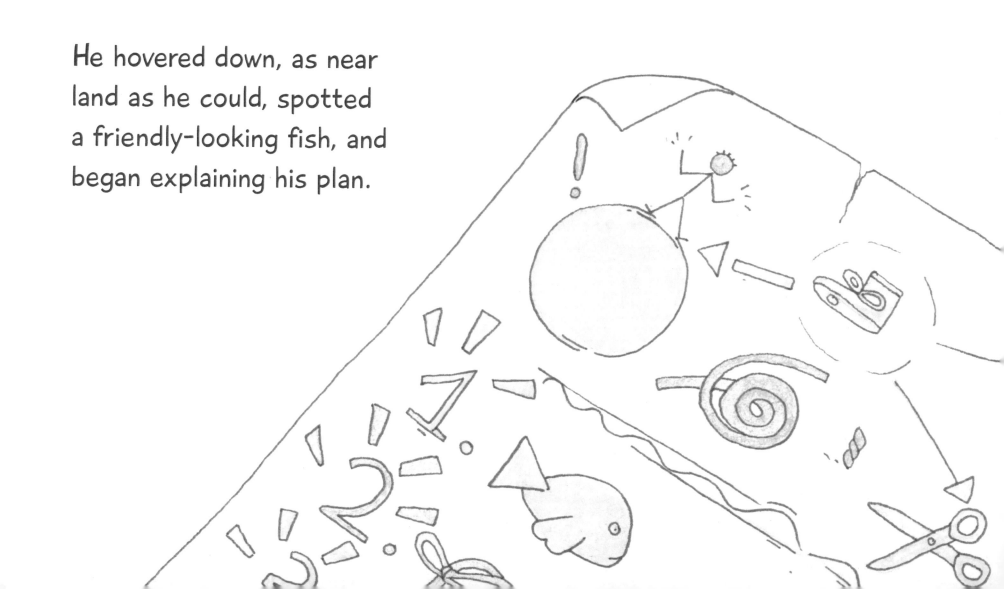

Fish don't talk, as some things never change. However, they are good listeners. As the fish listened intently, it nodded to agree with helping Nathan carry out his devious plan.

Nathan planned to tie ropes around his feet and slide those ropes through holes in the soles of his shoes. The fish would then hold onto those ropes and jump into a hole underground to be able to pull Nathan close enough to the ground. It would appear as if he were standing on land.

Nathan could not wait to execute his plan. He chose a nice place, right below a famous hang-out joint, so all the girls could see him and scream in fright.

He was ready.

The fish jumped into the hole.
It pulled the ropes down as it went.

At this point, Nathan was two inches away from the ground, and he was ecstatic as it was a magical feeling to be so close to something so impossible.

He started calling out to the people as he beamed with excitement. Now as much as the people would have liked to ignore Nathan, as they usually did, this time, they sure did notice him and even stared at him!

He had finally seemed to deserve their attention. How was he doing that? Were his feet actually on the ground?

Unfortunately for Nathan, the little fishy underground was beginning to get rather bored by everything. It decided to dig deeper until it found anything to tie Nathan's ropes on.

Fishy finally did
find something.
It was BIG,
it was shiny,
it was black,
and it was metallic.
In other words,
it was perfect.

Fishy tied the ropes
to it nice and tight.

It then dug its way back
up from a safe distance
away from Nathan.
Fish are cunning.

Here is where the story starts to make sense. As these humans, they all had magnetic properties

That big, shiny, black, metallic object was one of the millions of magnets covering the entire earth, just beneath the soil. It's what repelled the people, and kept them afloat.

Nathan had had his fun, and it was time to fly back up and laugh at everyone for falling for his antics once again.
He tugged at the ropes.
No response.
He tugged again.
There was still nothing.
"Strong fish," he thought to himself.

He kept tugging, but in a few minutes, he had to face the fact that he was stuck and, more importantly, needed help.

He cried out to the people, explaining his joke to them while begging for forgiveness simultaneously.

Angry at first, the crowd, quickly enough, changed to worried, as Nathan was but a child after all.

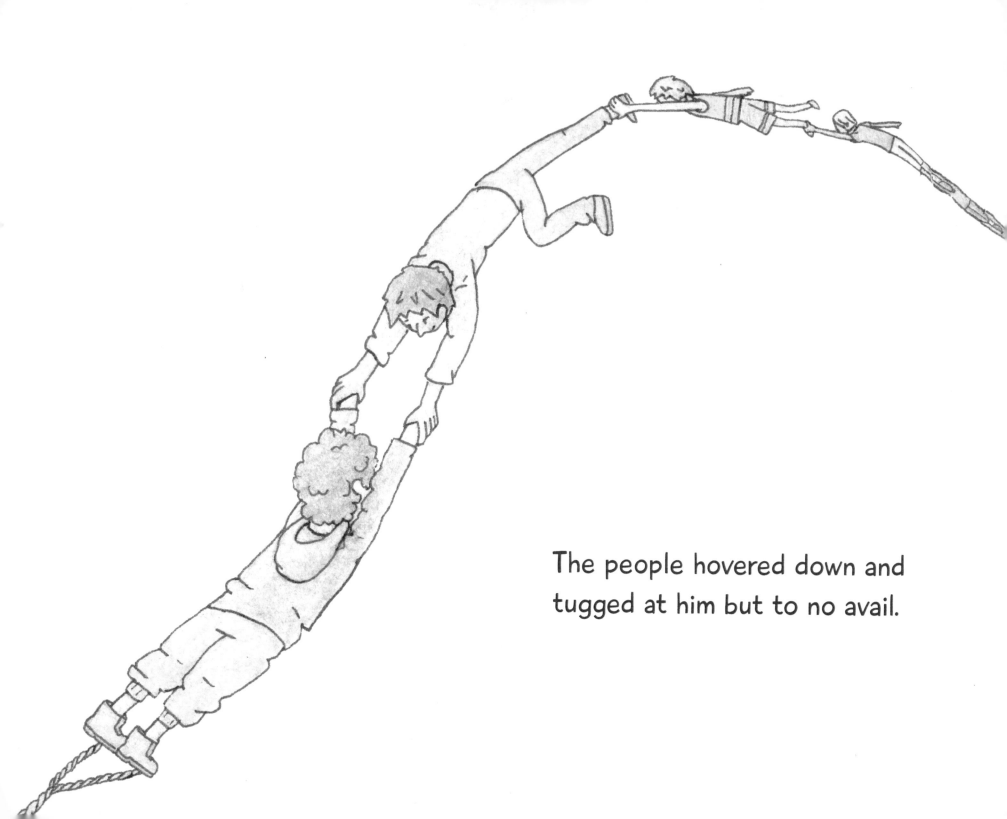

The people hovered down and tugged at him but to no avail.

The situation seemed to call for more strength. Within seconds, a line of people, one after the other, was formed in the sky. They all tugged at once.

THUD! And now their lives had changed forever. At this exact moment, when they freed Nathan, the magnet below got flipped over, causing every other magnet in the world to flip over in a domino effect.

While each and every person
flying around fell to the ground.
Some scared tried jumping back
up, only to fall back down again.
Others stumbled around like
toddlers.

But no matter what confusion these people were going through, they all felt unstoppable happiness. There lay a pile of disoriented people on top of an injured Nathan.

After they realized what had just happened, they all burst into smiles.

Nathan had the biggest smile among everyone, as he now felt responsible for this beautiful phenomenon. He was glad to accept the praise bestowed upon him!

Perhaps a time will come when these people will want to fly again, but not on that day and not any day soon. However, even if they ever want to fly again, they can't, as now flying is impossible.

Or is it?
Maybe we only need to dig a little deeper!